A happy family is number one.

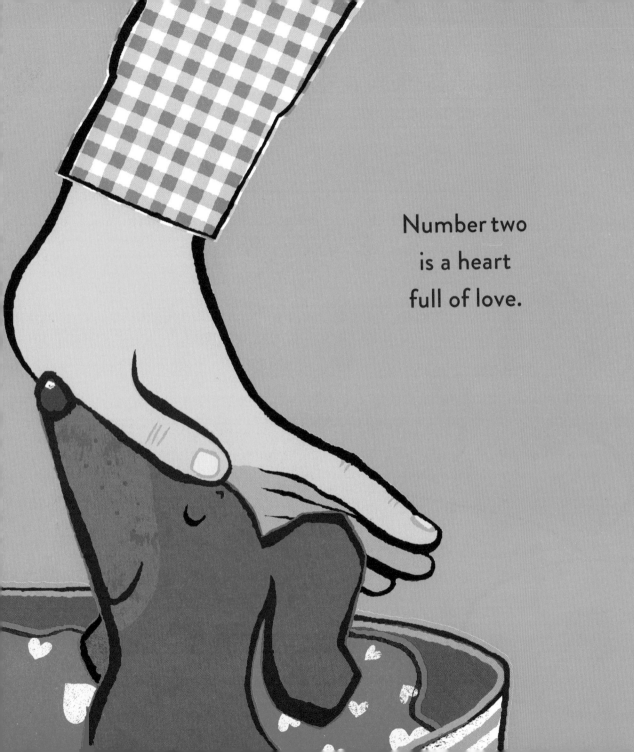

Number two
is a heart
full of love.

Playing together is number three.

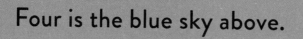

Four is the blue sky above.

Five is the joy of being alive.

Six is your paw in mine.

Seven is hearing
the rain outside.

Eight is the
warm sunshine.

Good food
to eat is
number nine.

Ten is your kiss goodnight.

And as the day ends,
being with you
makes everything feel right.

We've counted our blessings from one to ten;
there are many more to come.